09/2020

PALM BEACH COUNTY
LIBRARY SYSTEM
3650 Summit Boulevard
West Palm Beach, FL 33406-4198

A THIEF AT THE NATIONAL ZOO

by **Ron Roy**

illustrated by **Timothy Bush**

A STEPPING STONE BOOK™

Random House New York

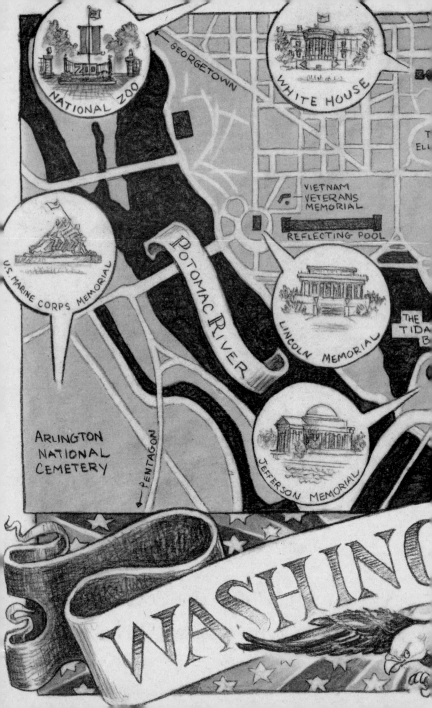

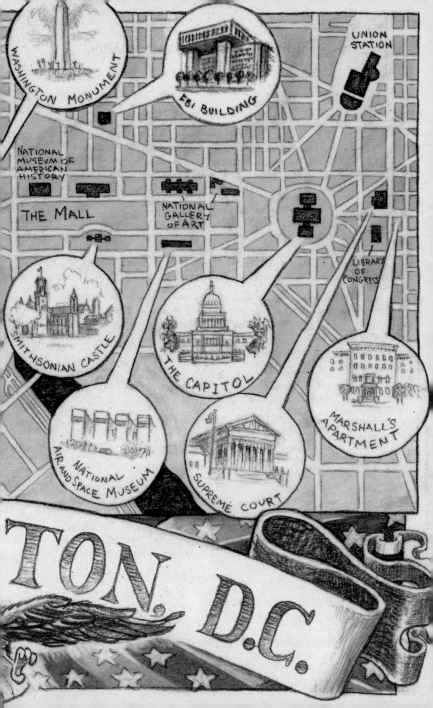

This is for my niece, Desiree Roy.
—R.R.

Photo credits: pp. 88–89, tiger images copyright © Corel Corporation;
p. 89 top, courtesy of the Library of Congress.

This is a work of fiction. Names, characters, places, and incidents either
are the product of the author's imagination or are used fictitiously. Any
resemblance to actual persons, living or dead, events, or locales is entirely
coincidental.

Text copyright © 2007 by Ron Roy
Illustrations copyright © 2007 by Timothy Bush
Cover illustration copyright © 2009 by Greg Swearingen

All rights reserved. Published in the United States by Random House
Children's Books, a division of Random House, Inc., New York.

Random House and the colophon are registered trademarks and A Stepping
Stone Book and the colophon are trademarks of Random House, Inc.

Visit us on the Web!
www.steppingstonesbooks.com
www.randomhouse.com/kids

Educators and librarians, for a variety of teaching tools, visit us at
www.randomhouse.com/teachers

Library of Congress Cataloging-in-Publication Data
Roy, Ron.
A thief at the National Zoo / by Ron Roy ; illustrated by Timothy Bush.
    p.   cm. — (Capital mysteries ; 9)
"Stepping Stone book."
Summary: KC and Marshall investigate the theft of a precious emerald,
brought by representatives of the Chinese government to bring luck to two
baby tigers born at the National Zoo.
ISBN 978-0-375-84804-9 (pbk.) — ISBN 978-0-375-94804-6 (lib. bdg.)
[1. Tigers—Fiction. 2. Stealing—Fiction. 3. National Zoological Park (U.S.)—
Fiction. 4. Washington (D.C.)—Fiction. 5. Mystery and detective stories.]
I. Bush, Timothy, ill. II. Title.
PZ7.R8139Tgt 2007   [Fic]—dc22   2007021739

Printed in the United States of America
13   12   11

Random House Children's Books supports the First Amendment and
celebrates the right to read.

Contents

1

The Tiger's Eye

"Here they are," Dirk, the zookeeper, said. He placed a small tiger cub in KC's lap and handed another cub to Marshall, KC's best friend. "They've just eaten, so they should fall asleep."

"Thank you," KC said. Then she sneezed. Twice.

"Are you allergic to cats?" Dirk asked KC. He was tall and his long arms were tanned. He wore a short-sleeved shirt and cargo pants with zippered pockets. A thin silver bracelet dangled around one wrist.

KC sneezed again. "No, we have three cats at home and they never make me sneeze," she said. "But maybe I'm allergic to tigers!"

Dirk laughed. "See you in twenty minutes," he said. "I need to check on mama tiger." He left the room and closed the door.

The tiger cub on KC's lap opened its mouth and yawned. The two-month-old Sumatran tiger was the size of one of KC's cats.

"You are so cute!" KC said, tickling the drowsy tiger's belly.

"Gee, thanks, KC. You're kind of cute, too," said Marshall with a grin.

"Not you!" KC said. "I mean little Lucy here."

"Lucy is a dumb name for a tiger," Marshall commented. "I mean, I guess it's okay for a tiny cub. But can you see calling a five-hundred-pound tiger Lucy?"

KC Corcoran and Marshall Li were at the National Zoo in Washington, D.C. Their friend Dr. Phillip Tutu was the zoo's head veterinarian. He had invited them to play with the baby Sumatran tigers in a small room across from the tiger enclosure.

"Ricky is a pretty silly name, too," KC said. Lucy's twin brother, Ricky, was curled up on Marshall's lap. "But in a little while they'll get their real names."

"Tell me again about this party tonight," Marshall said.

"A rich family from China is coming here to donate a lot of money to the zoo to help the tigers," KC said. "They have a daughter who's twelve. She gets to pick names for the tigers."

"Cool. Maybe she'll name this little guy Fang," Marshall said.

KC shook her head. "The president said she's giving them special Sumatran names," she said. KC's stepfather, Zachary Thornton, was the President of the United States. She lived in the White House with him and her mom.

Marshall looked at the sleeping tiger cub in his lap. "Where is Sumatra, anyway?" he asked.

"Somewhere in Indonesia. It's part of Asia," KC said. "I found it on the big map in my room."

The door opened again and Dr. Tutu stepped inside. He wore a loose shirt and crisp white pants. He was carrying a leather briefcase in one hand and a half-eaten apple in the other.

"How are you two getting along with these famous babies?" he asked. He set his briefcase on the floor.

"Fine," KC said. "So far all they want to do is sleep."

Dr. Tutu laughed. "You're lucky," he said. "When they wake up, they'll be running all over the place."

Dr. Tutu moved aside. A girl with dark hair was standing behind him. "KC and Marshall, say hello to Sunwoo Chu," he said. "All the way from China."

The girl was a little bit taller than KC. She wore a T-shirt, dark blue shorts, and sandals on her feet.

"Hello, I am happy to meet you," Sunwoo said. She sat on the floor next to KC. "My father and your stepfather are having a meeting at the White House

5

today. They will talk about how to help save tigers from extinction."

Marshall gave Ricky a pat on the head. "It's hard to think of the world with no tigers," he said.

"My father and President Thornton are trying to find ways to make the people happy, and the tigers as well," Sunwoo said. "Perhaps the Tiger's Eye will bring luck."

"What's the Tiger's Eye?" KC asked.

"A special magic jewel," answered Sunwoo. She nodded at the baby tigers. "May I hold one, please?"

"Sure." Marshall transferred Ricky to Sunwoo's lap. The little cub opened its eyes, then let out a small growl.

"Oh, I'm sorry I disturbed your nap!" Sunwoo said.

The tiger growled again, making the kids laugh.

"Just a few more minutes," Dr. Tutu said. He picked up his briefcase and walked toward the door. "We have to return Ricky and Lucy to their mama across the hall."

"Um, what's this magic jewel?" asked Marshall after Dr. Tutu, chomping on his apple, had left the room.

Sunwoo stroked the tiger's belly. "It is a legend in my country," she said. "Two thousand years ago, a Chinese boy was digging roots to help feed his hungry brothers and sisters. Their parents had died, and the children were alone. Buried in the dirt beneath a tree, he discovered a smooth ball of amber. The amber was the color of light tea, and the boy could see something inside. It was an emerald."

"What's amber?" Marshall asked.

"It is like sap that comes from a pine tree," Sunwoo said. "Over time, it hardens like plastic."

"So this emerald got covered in this sap stuff, then it hardened?" KC asked.

Sunwoo nodded. "But it's very, very rare," she said. "No one thought emeralds and amber came from the same place. And neither is found in China. It's a mystery. Or maybe the legend is not true." Sunwoo shrugged.

"How big is this Tiger's Eye?" Marshall asked Sunwoo.

She made a circle with her fingers. "Like a peach," she said. "But inside, instead of the pit, there is an emerald."

"Cool!" Marshall said.

"The boy raced home with the beautiful thing he had found," Sunwoo went on. "The people in his town came to see the emerald. When they saw how poor and sick the children were, they brought food and money. His brothers and sisters became strong and healthy. The boy himself grew up to become the mayor of his village. He made sure that no one ever went hungry again. He told everyone that he owed his good fortune to the Tiger's Eye emerald."

"What happened to the emerald?" Marshall asked.

"It has been passed down from generation to generation," Sunwoo said. "It has always brought health and luck. The premier of China gave the Tiger's Eye to my father to bring here. He will lend it to the zoo for one year. It will bring good luck to your people, but especially to the tigers."

The door opened and Dirk came in. He was talking to someone on a walkie-talkie. He finished and clipped the device to his belt. "Time for them to go back," he said.

KC placed Lucy in Dirk's hand. She sneezed. Dirk scooped up Ricky in his other hand.

"The cubs are beautiful," Sunwoo said as Dirk took them away. "I have perfect names for them! Now I must leave. My mother and father are waiting to take me sightseeing."

"We have to get home, too," KC said.

The kids left the room. They were in a long hallway with a wall on one side and tall, wide doors on the other.

"Excuse me, but I don't know the way,"

Sunwoo said. "Dr. Tutu brought me here, but I was not paying attention."

"We'll show you," KC said. "This hallway runs under the spaces where the lions and tigers live."

"What's in there?" Sunwoo asked. A door stood directly across from the room they'd just left. A number 3 was painted on the door, below a small window.

"Take a look," Marshall said.

Sunwoo stood on her tiptoes and peeked through the thick glass window. "Goodness, this is where the tigers live!" she cried, jumping away from the door.

Marshall laughed. "Don't worry, it's locked," he said. He put his hand on the knob and twisted. The door didn't budge.

The three kids walked down the long passageway. They passed several more doors, each with a window and a number painted in black. At the end, Marshall opened a normal-looking door into the public part of the zoo.

"Where are you staying?" KC asked. "We can walk you back to your hotel."

"Thank you, but my father's driver is waiting out front." She looked around and giggled. "Where is the front?"

"Follow me!" Marshall said. He led them past the tiger enclosure. They stopped to look at the huge mother tiger. She was lying next to her twin cubs.

"Can you believe little Lucy and Ricky will grow up to look like that?" Marshall said.

They watched the tiger and her cubs for a few more minutes, then walked down paths past other animal exhibits to a

gate. "Is this where you came in?" KC asked.

"I think so," Sunwoo said. "Oh, there's my driver!"

Sunwoo shook hands with KC and Marshall. "I will see you tonight!" she said.

Sunwoo passed through the gate and walked up to a white stretch limo. The driver, dressed in a dark suit, opened the rear door for her.

KC and Marshall watched the stretch limo leave.

"Wish we had one of those," Marshall said.

"Not me. I like riding on the Metro trains," KC said. She pulled her subway ticket out of a pocket. "And that's where we have to go now. We have a party to get ready for!"

2

Creepy Fingers in the Dark

At seven o'clock, KC and Marshall were back at the zoo. They came with the president and KC's mom, Lois, in a presidential car. Two other cars followed. Each held four secret service agents.

The president was wearing a tuxedo. Lois wore a long white dress. A flower was tucked into her hair.

KC and Marshall wore their best dress-up clothes.

Dr. Tutu was waiting at the entrance of the zoo. He had dressed in a black tuxedo and white shirt. He carried his leather briefcase.

"Good evening, Mr. and Mrs. President," Dr. Tutu said. He escorted them, and the president's secret service agents, through the empty zoo to a room near where KC and Marshall had played with the tiger cubs.

There were about twenty-five well-dressed people already there. Waiters carried trays of food and drinks across a thick red carpet. A crystal chandelier cast a soft light. Music came from a pair of speakers mounted on the walls.

When the president and Lois entered, everyone clapped. The secret service agents moved into the room and stood where they could keep an eye on the president and his family.

"Look, KC, there's Sunwoo and her parents," Marshall said.

Sunwoo and her mother wore matching yellow dresses. Sunwoo had a small purse with a thin gold chain slung over one shoulder. Her father was dressed in a tuxedo, like most of the men in the room.

"Let's go say hi," KC said.

KC and Marshall walked across the deep carpet. Sunwoo saw them coming and smiled.

"Mother, Father, these are my new friends," Sunwoo said. "KC and Marshall, these are my parents, Mr. and Mrs. Chu."

They all shook hands.

"I enjoyed my meeting with your stepfather," Mr. Chu told KC. He winked. "And I like your big White House!"

Marshall glanced around the room. "Is the Tiger's Eye here?" he whispered to Sunwoo.

Sunwoo nodded. "Father, I told them about it," she said. "Can you show them?"

Sunwoo's father was carrying a small black box with a tiger painted on the lid. Mr. Chu opened the lid and removed a square of red silk.

Nestled at the bottom of the box was a round yellowish object the size of a baseball. The roughly shaped emerald inside seemed to float in the amber.

KC stared at the emerald through the amber covering. The green gem appeared to glow. She had never seen anything so old or mysterious.

"Is it worth a lot of money?" Marshall asked.

"To the Chinese people, the Tiger's Eye is priceless," Mr. Chu said. "We would not sell it for all the money in the world."

Dr. Tutu approached Sunwoo's father. "If you're ready, Mr. Chu," he said.

Dr. Tutu led Mr. Chu to a corner of the room, where a table stood near the door. A velvet cloth lay in the center of the table. Mr. Chu placed the black box on the cloth. Dr. Tutu set his briefcase on the floor and nudged it under the table with his foot.

"Good evening, everyone," Dr. Tutu said. "We are here tonight to accept a generous gift from this gentleman, Mr. Chien Chu. As you all know, many species of tigers are now extinct or endangered. Mr. Chu's gift will help this zoo find more ways to protect the world's tigers. Mr. Chu has also brought a surprise from his country." All eyes went to the black box on the table.

"But first, Mr. Chu's daughter, Sunwoo, will give the tiger cubs their official names," Dr. Tutu added. He motioned for Sunwoo to join him and her father.

Everyone in the room smiled and looked at Sunwoo.

"Come up there with me," Sunwoo whispered to KC and Marshall. "This is very embarrassing!"

KC looked at Marshall and nodded. They joined Sunwoo next to the table.

Dr. Tutu pulled a walkie-talkie from a clip on his belt and spoke into it. A moment later, the door opened and Dirk came in carrying Lucy and Ricky. He stood behind KC, holding the cubs so everyone could see their cute faces.

KC felt a sneeze coming on. Maybe she was allergic to tigers after all! She held her breath and squeezed her eyes shut. *Please,* she thought, *don't let me sneeze now in the middle of the ceremony!*

There were a lot of oohs and aahs as the guests admired the baby Sumatran tigers.

Dr. Tutu smiled at Sunwoo. "Have you picked names?" he asked.

"Yes," Sunwoo said. "My family has chosen Indonesian names, because these are Sumatran tigers. The boy tiger will be Guntur. That is the Indonesian word for 'thunder.' We have named the girl Melati, which means 'jasmine blossom.'"

Everyone clapped again.

"Those are fine names," Dr. Tutu said. "Thank you, Sunwoo, for—"

Suddenly the lights went out and the room was pitch-black.

For a few seconds there was total silence, then everyone began talking at once. "I can't see anything!" one woman cried. "What should we do?"

"Please remain calm," Dr. Tutu called out into the black room. "We seem to have lost power, but I'm sure it will be back on in a moment."

Just as KC turned to say something to Marshall, someone bumped into her, nearly knocking her off her feet. She reached out in the dark, trying to keep from falling.

She felt the table, then her fingers touched a human hand. Startled, she pulled her own hands back. Then she sneezed three times in a row.

Next to KC, Dr. Tutu began speaking to someone through his walkie-talkie. KC heard people moving about, jostling each other in the dark. A few people were laughing, like this was a party game.

KC heard some of the secret service agents urgently talking to each other about POTUS. *POTUS* was their code word for her stepfather. The letters stood for "President of the United States."

KC had a scary thought. What if the lights going out were part of a kidnapping plot?

"What's going on?" Marshall said into KC's ear.

"Beats me," KC answered. "Just stand still or you'll get trampled!"

The lights came back on.

KC blinked in the sudden brightness. She looked up and saw Dirk holding Ricky and Lucy, one in each big hand.

They were squirming and hissing. Their little legs were clawing the air.

KC turned around and tried to find her mother and the president. She spotted them near a far wall, totally surrounded by secret service agents. KC's mother waved.

Sunwoo stood between her parents. "What happened?" she asked her father.

"Just a power failure," Mr. Chu said. He patted his daughter's hand.

"Now you see why we need your donations!" Dr. Tutu joked to the crowd.

Everyone laughed.

"Before the lights went out, I was going to ask Mr. Chu to tell us about his special surprise," Dr. Tutu continued.

Mr. Chu placed his hand on the black box. He told everyone how the amber-covered emerald had been found two thousand years ago. "When visitors come to China, they want to see the Great Wall first. Then they go to the Imperial Palace to see this Tiger's Eye."

Mr. Chu placed his hand on the box. "I brought it to Washington, D.C., to bring luck to the people," he said. "Then the people will bring luck to the tigers."

Mr. Chu lifted the box lid, facing it toward the crowd so everyone could see the Tiger's Eye.

KC looked at the box. Except for the small silk cloth, it was empty.

Someone giggled nervously.

Dr. Tutu and Mr. Chu stared into the box. To KC, they seemed frozen, as if they'd been playing statues.

"The Tiger's Eye is gone!" Mr. Chu said.

3
KC Remembers

Everyone started talking at once.

The president walked to the middle of the room. "Folks, may I have your attention?" he said in a loud but gentle voice. "Please, everyone, be calm. Please stay in the room until we get this sorted out."

The president, Mr. Chu, and Dr. Tutu stepped into the hallway. The president leaned against the door, holding it open. KC watched them talking in whispers.

Soon the three men came back into the room. Dirk was still holding the wriggling tiger cubs. He mumbled to Dr. Tutu. KC thought she heard him ask something about the cubs. Dr. Tutu nodded, and he and Dirk left the room together.

Before the door closed behind them, KC saw Dr. Tutu unlock door number 3 across the hall. In a couple of minutes, the two men came back without Ricky and Lucy.

"I know this is going to be annoying," the president said to the group. "But this room and everyone in it will have to be searched."

Several of the guests groaned. "I have a babysitter!" one woman said.

"This won't take long," the president promised. "The First Lady and I will be searched along with everyone else. Even my secret service agents will have to be checked. Please be patient. We'll all be on our way home soon."

The door opened as the president stopped speaking. Five people dressed in gray uniforms stepped inside. ID badges hung from chains around their necks. The word SECURITY was stitched into patches on their shirtfronts.

"What are we looking for, Mr. President?" a guard asked.

"Mr. Chu, please tell us," the president said.

Mr. Chu described the Tiger's Eye, and the guards went to work. They asked the men to line up on one side and the women on the other. The guards began searching everyone.

"Will we have to get undressed?" Marshall whispered to the president.

KC giggled.

The president laughed. "No, Marshall,"

he said. "They'll just pat us all down. The Tiger's Eye isn't exactly tiny. If anyone has hidden it in their clothing, these folks will find it."

KC and her mother joined the women being searched. The president and Marshall went with the men. They were in line behind Dirk and Mr. Chu. The secret service agents kept the president in sight at all times.

Twenty minutes later, every person in the room had been searched. The Tiger's Eye had not been found.

One of the security guards made a list of everyone's name, address, and phone number. Then the people were allowed to leave.

KC stood with her mom, waiting for the president. He was talking to Mr. Chu. The president had his hand on Mr. Chu's shoulder, speaking quietly. Sunwoo's father looked very angry. KC would have given anything to know what was being said.

KC had a strong feeling that searching the guests had been a waste of time. No thief would be dumb enough to hide the valuable Chinese emerald in his clothing.

She glanced around, checking for a window. She'd read a book once about a robber in a jewelry store tossing a bag of diamonds through a window. His partner had been waiting outside to catch the loot.

KC saw a couple of sofas and chairs and a few small tables. Now that there were fewer people in the room, KC also noticed a fish aquarium standing against one wall. But there were no windows.

The president, surrounded again by his

secret service agents, walked over. "I guess we can go now," he said. "After we leave, the security staff is going to search this room thoroughly. Dr. Tutu and I told them to take the walls down and the floor boards up if they have to!"

The next morning, Marshall got to the White House at eight-thirty. The guards all knew him, so he was allowed upstairs to the president's private residence.

KC was eating cereal when he walked into the kitchen.

"Good morning, Marshall," Yvonne, the president's maid, said. "Have you had breakfast?"

"No," Marshall said. "KC told me to be here so early, I had to run out of the house!"

"Have some cereal," KC said. She tapped her spoon against the box of Animal Fruiteez sitting in the middle of the table next to a basket of fruit.

Yvonne brought him a bowl and spoon and a glass of orange juice. Marshall poured cereal and milk into his bowl. He began poking through the little floating animals with his spoon.

"What're you looking for?" KC asked.

"One shaped like a spider," Marshall said.

Marshall loved any animal, but especially those with six or eight legs.

"Marsh, there are no spider shapes," KC reminded him. "Fruiteez are all circus animals, remember?"

Marshall kept peering at the floating shapes. "Aha!" he said. He grabbed a

shape and held it up. "No spiders, eh? So what's this?"

KC shook her head. "It's a chimpanzee, Marsh," she said.

Marshall popped the chimp into his mouth. "So why did you make me get out of bed so early?" he asked.

"I've been thinking about the missing jewel," KC said.

"You mean the security guys didn't find it yet?"

KC shook her head. "I don't think so. And the president made a bunch of phone calls to China last night." She gestured toward the president's study. "I think he's talking to Mr. Chu right now."

Marshall swallowed a mouthful of Fruiteez. "So what did they say?"

"Marshall, I don't listen to other

people's private phone calls!" KC said.

"You don't?" Marshall asked with big eyes.

KC wanted to be a TV anchorperson when she grew up. She was preparing herself by reading newspapers, watching news on TV, and being extra observant.

KC sighed. "Well, I did hear a few things," she admitted. "By accident!" she added as Marshall gave her another look. "I think the president was talking to the premier of China. The president promised he'd find the Tiger's Eye, even if he had to call out the National Guard."

Marshall gulped some orange juice. "Maybe the thief swallowed it," he said. "I saw a movie once where some crook swallowed a gold ring."

"Marsh, the Tiger's Eye is too big," KC

said. She grabbed an apple from the fruit bowl. "It was bigger than this!"

She got up and began pacing around the kitchen. "We both saw the Tiger's Eye in the box, right?"

"Right," Marshall said, still eating his cereal.

"And the only time anyone could have taken it out of the box was when the lights went out," she went on.

"Right," Marshall repeated. "But the room was totally dark. How would anyone be able to find a black box in a black room?" He took the last sip of his orange juice. "Do you think the crook knew the lights were going to go out?"

"How could he know?" KC asked. "Unless . . ."

"Unless he knew that someone else

was going to make the lights go out!" Marshall said. "Someone who wasn't in the room!"

KC stared at Marshall. "Of course," she said. "The thief was working with a partner!"

"They must've planned the whole thing in advance," Marshall said. "They had to know about the Chus, the emerald, the party last night, everything!"

KC was staring at her Fruiteez box.

Marshall snapped his fingers in front of her face. "KC? Anyone home?"

KC looked at him. "I think I touched him in the dark," she said quietly.

"Who?" Marshall asked.

"When the lights went out, someone smacked into me," KC told Marshall. "I grabbed for the table to keep from falling.

I felt someone's hand in the dark. At the time, I didn't think much about it. But now I think it was the thief's hand. I touched him when he was reaching for the black box!"

"Wow!" Marshall said. "Was it a man or a woman's hand?"

KC shook her head. "It could have been either, I guess," she said. "I just know my fingers touched skin, so I backed away."

Marshall nodded. "So, we know the crook had skin," he said wisely.

"Very funny, Marsh," KC said.

"So now what?" Marshall asked.

KC made a decision. She grabbed Marshall by the arm. "Let's go," she said.

"Go where?"

"To the scene of the crime!" KC said.

4

The Scene of the Crime

"Why are we going back there?" Marshall asked.

KC scribbled a note for her mom and grabbed her backpack.

"I have a plan," KC said. The kids left the kitchen, waved to Arnold, the marine guard, and hurried toward the exit.

"Okay, what's the plan?" Marshall asked as they headed toward the Metro train that would take them to the National Zoo.

"We'll figure out how to shut off the lights, then re-create the crime," KC said.

"Like on TV?" Marshall asked.

KC nodded.

"But those TV stories are fake, KC, and this is real," Marshall said. "Besides, how are you going to get all those people to come back?"

"I'm not," KC said. "It's just going to be me and you. You'll be the crook, and I'll do what I did last night when the crook bumped into me in the dark. Maybe we'll remember something important that happened while the lights were out."

"Oh brother," Marshall said.

A half hour later, they walked through the zoo's front entrance. KC and Marshall hurried past the pandas, the elephants, and the wolves to the tiger enclosure. They slipped through the back door and made their way to the room where the party had been.

"Wow," Marshall said.

The furniture had been taken away. The stereo speakers had been taken down from the walls. Dangling wires were all that were left.

The red carpet had been rolled up and was lying against one wall. The only other things in the room were the fish tank, one chair, and the same small table that had held the black box.

The table was now next to the fish tank. Someone had taken all the rocks and fake plants out of the tank and left them on the table.

Inside the tank there were a few tropical fish. They swam around, probably wondering what happened to their rocks and plants.

"Looks like someone even searched

this tank," KC said. "Help me move this stuff."

KC and Marshall placed the rocks and plants on the floor. KC examined each rock carefully. Then they carried the table to where it had been standing last night.

"Okay, pretend you're Mr. Chu," KC said. "Put the black box on the table."

"You told me I was the crook," said Marshall.

"Just please cooperate, okay?" KC said. "Where's the black box, Mr. Chu?"

Marshall shook his head. Then he pretended to pull a box out of thin air. "Why, it's right here, Miss Corcoran!"

"Thank you, Mr. Chu!" KC said. "Now put it on the table."

Marshall did as she ordered. He mimed placing the box on the table.

"Go shut off the lights," KC said.

"Are you talking to me, the crook, or Mr. Chu?" Marshall asked.

KC giggled. "I'm talking to you," she said.

Marshall headed for the light switch, which was by the room's only door.

"Wait a sec," Marshall said. "At breakfast, we agreed that someone outside the room had to shut off the lights. But there's a switch right here. It could have been someone in the room!"

Marshall flipped the switch, and the room grew dark. He hit the switch again, and the lights came on.

KC stared at the light switch. "Do you remember anyone standing over there when the lights went out?" she asked.

Marshall shook his head. "I think I saw

one of the secret service agents here by the door, but I'm not sure," he said.

"Okay, shut them off again," KC said. "Then pretend you're the crook. Come to the table, open the box, and take the jewel."

"There is no box," Marshall said with a grin.

"Just please do it, okay?" KC said.

Marshall plunged the room into darkness again. KC positioned herself where she had been standing last night. She put her hands out, as she had when she touched the thief's hand.

She heard Marshall's feet on the wood floor. "Are you here yet?" she asked him.

"How am I supposed to know?" Marshall yelped. "I can't see the stupid table, and I can't see the stupid box!"

"Walk toward my voice," KC said. "When you feel the table, reach for the box."

A few seconds later, KC felt Marshall bump into the edge of the table.

"Okay, I'm here," Marshall muttered. "And I feel like a jerk."

"Are you reaching for the box?" KC asked.

"Reaching," Marshall muttered.

Suddenly KC felt one of Marshall's hands brush against her own. She pulled her hand back, as she had last night.

"Okay?" Marshall asked. "Can I turn the lights on?"

"Not yet," KC said. "Last night, something else happened, but I can't remember what. It was right after I touched that creepy hand."

"Well, I'm not standing in the dark all day while you—"

Just then the lights went on again. KC turned toward the door, and there was Dr. Tutu. He was holding his briefcase.

"Well, hello," he said to KC and Marshall. "What are you doing here?"

KC thought of about ten excuses, but decided to go with the truth. "We were trying to figure out how someone could have stolen the emerald in the dark."

Dr. Tutu looked at the table. Then he glanced at the fish tank and the rocks and plants on the floor.

"And did you figure it out?" Dr. Tutu asked.

KC shook her head.

Dr. Tutu smiled. "My staff and I have been doing the same thing," he said. "I

even thought the thief might have dropped the thing into the fish tank. But as you can see, that didn't happen."

"Maybe the crook sneaked out of the room in the dark," Marshall said.

Dr. Tutu shook his head. "I don't think so. When the lights went out, I walked over and stood in front of the door," he said. "Nobody came past me."

KC blinked. *Unless* you *are the crook, Dr. Tutu,* she thought. *You could have zipped out of the room, then slipped back in again.*

"Um, we were wondering if the crook was working with someone else," Marshall said. "See, we thought the partner turned off the lights from outside the room."

"I believe that is exactly what happened," Dr. Tutu said. "As you can see, it's also possible to turn them off from that wall switch. But since the music went off when the lights did last night, I have to guess that it was done from the main power board."

Dr. Tutu stared at KC and Marshall. It looked as if he was trying to make a decision.

Finally he opened his briefcase and slid out a sheet of paper with typing on it.

"I faxed a copy of this to President Thornton," Dr. Tutu said. He held it out toward KC. "Don't be afraid to touch it. We already checked for fingerprints."

"What is it?" KC asked, reaching for the paper.

"A ransom note," he said. "Our thief in the dark wants a million dollars."

5

Million-Dollar Ransom

KC read the words while Marshall looked over her shoulder.

IF YOU WANT THE TIGER'S EYE, WIRE ONE MILLION DOLLARS TO THIS ACCOUNT NUMBER AT ISLAND BANK ON GRAND CAYMAN.

RX70933342-246

IF THE MONEY IS NOT IN THAT ACCOUNT WITHIN 24 HOURS, YOU WILL NEVER SEE THE EMERALD AGAIN.

"What does he mean, wire the money?" Marshall asked.

"Whoever wrote this note has a bank account in Grand Cayman," Dr. Tutu said. "That's one of the Caribbean Islands. If we go along with his plan, a bank here in Washington will send a message to his account there. Within minutes, the thief will be one million dollars richer. It's sort of like sending money in an e-mail."

"Why couldn't the cops just wait for the crook to get the money, then go there and arrest him?" Marshall asked.

Dr. Tutu shook his head. "In this country, we could do that," he said. "But not in the Cayman Islands. Bank accounts there are totally private. That means we can't learn who opened the account, and we can't get at the money."

KC handed the note back to Dr. Tutu. "Where did you get that?" she asked him.

Dr. Tutu put the ransom note back into his briefcase and set the case on the floor behind the table.

"I found it slipped under the door of my office this morning," he said. "I got there at eight o'clock. The thief left the note either very late last night or before eight this morning."

Dr. Tutu stared at the fish swimming around in the tank.

"The lights were only out for about a minute," KC said. "Marshall and I think the thief had to be standing pretty near the table."

"I was closer to the table than anyone," Dr. Tutu said. "Do you suspect me?"

KC felt herself blushing. She nodded. "We didn't know what to think," she admitted. "Now I don't think it was you!"

"Thank you," Dr. Tutu said. He smiled for the first time since he came in.

"Dirk was standing near the table, too," Marshall said. "Or maybe one of the waiters was close enough, so when the lights went out, he could grab the thing."

"But Dirk had his hands full of the tiger cubs, and the waiters were carrying trays of food and drinks," Dr. Tutu said. "I'm afraid the police think I am the most likely choice, because I had nothing in my hands."

"Are they going to arrest you?" KC asked.

"I don't know," Dr. Tutu said. "They questioned me last night and took my fingerprints."

"Why'd they take your fingerprints?" Marshall asked.

"To compare them with prints they found on the box," he said.

"But you didn't touch the box," KC said. "Only Mr. Chu did."

"I did, too, I'm afraid." Dr. Tutu shook his head. "When the room suddenly went dark, I reached out and placed my hand on the box," he said. "I wanted to make sure it was still there. Then I went and stood in front of the door."

KC felt confused. If Dr. Tutu admitted he had touched the box when the lights were out, maybe it had been his hand she had felt—and not the thief's hand. Or maybe he was lying about why he touched the box. Could Dr. Tutu be the thief after all?

"Did the police search this room last night?" KC asked.

Dr. Tutu nodded. "We were all here till two o'clock in the morning."

KC was getting a headache. "So if the guests and the room were searched, then the thief must have hidden the emerald somewhere else, outside this room," she said.

"But Dr. Tutu said no one got past him at the door," Marshall reminded KC.

"You see the problem," Dr. Tutu said sadly. "Mr. Chu's treasure has simply disappeared. It's not in this room, and no one could have taken it out of the room."

6

The First Arrest

The door behind Dr. Tutu opened. Two police officers came into the room. "Dr. Phillip Tutu, please come with us to the police station," one of the officers said.

"I gave my statement last night," Dr. Tutu said. "I allowed my fingerprints to be taken. How else can I help you?"

The other officer stepped forward. "Your fingerprints were found on the box," he said. "Last night, you didn't mention touching it."

Dr. Tutu took a step backward. "I can explain that!" he said.

"I'm sure you'll be given a chance to do

just that," the taller officer said. "Now please come with us."

The officers escorted Dr. Tutu from the room. When one of them opened the door, KC saw Mr. Chu standing in the hallway.

"Thank you, officers," KC heard Mr. Chu say. Then he followed the officers down the hallway.

"I can't believe this!" Marshall cried. "Sunwoo's father thinks Dr. Tutu stole the emerald!"

"I have to call the president and tell him," KC said. "Come on, there's a phone in the gift shop across the path."

The kids left the tiger building and dashed over to the gift shop. KC was given permission to use the phone, and she dialed the president's private number.

"Busy," she said as she hung up. She tried again, but all she heard were more annoying busy sounds.

"He must be talking to China again," KC said.

"Or the bank in Grand Cayman," Marshall added.

KC tried the number a third time, got another busy signal, and gave up. She walked over to the gift-shop clerk, who was rearranging a row of stuffed panda bears on a shelf.

"Excuse me," KC said. "My friend and I are helping the president find something. I'm his stepdaughter, and I was—"

"I know who you are, dear," the woman said. "And all of us are just sick about what happened last night! How can I help you?"

"Can you tell us where the main electric power board is?" KC asked.

"Why, I believe it's in the security room," the clerk said. "It's that building over there."

KC thanked the woman. She nudged Marshall toward the door.

"Why are we going there?" Marshall asked.

"Dr. Tutu told us the lights were shut off from the main power board," KC said. "So maybe we can find out who was in the security room at seven-fifteen last night."

They came to a door with the words ROOM 15—SECURITY—KEEP OUT stenciled onto it.

KC knocked on the door.

"Who is it?" a muffled voice asked.

"Um, it's KC and Marshall," KC said.

The door swung open. A woman was standing there dressed in coveralls over a T-shirt. A wide leather belt was cinched around her waist. Tools, a cell phone, and a walkie-talkie hung from the belt. A chain around her neck held a plastic ID card. KC could see the woman's picture and her name, Connie, on the card.

"Who are you?" the woman asked KC and Marshall. She leaned against the door frame. A thin silver bracelet gleamed on her tanned arm.

"I'm KC Corcoran," KC said. "The president's stepdaughter."

Connie nodded. "Right. I know Dirk lets you play with the new cubs," she said. "What can I do for you?"

"Did you hear about the theft last

night?" KC asked. "When the lights went off?"

"Everyone on staff knows about it," Connie said. "Have they caught the guys who stole that emerald thing?"

"No, and we're trying to help find it," KC went on. "Dr. Tutu told us he thinks the lights might have been turned off from in there." She pointed into the room behind the woman.

Connie was shaking her head before KC finished. "Never happened," she said. "I was home last night, and my keys were with me. This room was locked up from six o'clock on, and only one other person on staff has a key."

"Who's that?" Marshall asked.

"Dr. Tutu," Connie said.

KC and Marshall stared at her.

"He just got arrested," KC said. "But we don't think he did it, so we're trying to help!"

"Dr. Tutu was arrested?" the woman said. "When?"

"Just five minutes ago," Marshall said. "Two police came. They said they found his fingerprints on the emerald box."

"I'm shocked," the woman said, shaking her head. "Well, good luck, kids." As she started to close the door, she added, "Say hi to the president for me."

KC and Marshall headed down the hallway. "We're missing something," KC said.

"What do you mean?" Marshall asked.

"Well, there's something weird about those lights going off," KC said. "Did someone in the room shut them off, or did someone sneak into that security room and do it? Or maybe it really was just a power outage."

"I'm beginning to think Dr. Tutu *is* guilty," Marshall said. "He could have given his key to his partner."

"Maybe," KC said. "And who did I touch when the lights went out? Was it Dr. Tutu or the crook reaching toward the box? Or is Dr. Tutu the crook?"

"But the biggest mystery is, where is the emerald now?" Marshall added. "Dr. Tutu said no one got past him at the door."

KC stopped in her tracks. "Wait a minute!" she said. "I just remembered! When Dirk took the cubs back to their mother, Dr. Tutu was with him. They went across the hall to room three before we all got searched!"

"So?" Marshall said. "Dr. Tutu had to unlock the door because Dirk had the cubs in his hands."

"Don't you see, Marsh? If Dr. Tutu is the thief, he could have hidden the emerald when he left the room," KC said. "Let's go ask Dirk if he noticed Dr. Tutu doing anything weird."

They stopped at room number 3. KC and Marshall peeked through the window. KC saw Dirk sweeping up some straw and throwing it into a trash barrel. The twin tiger cubs were on the floor by his feet, trying to attack the broom. The mother tiger was nowhere in sight.

KC knocked on the little window, but Dirk didn't turn around. KC knocked harder, but Dirk went on sweeping.

"He can't hear us," Marshall said.

"Okay, we'll ask him when he comes out," KC said. They went across the hall to wait. KC used a fish-tank rock to prop open the door.

Next to the table, they saw a leather briefcase standing on the floor.

"Dr. Tutu forgot it," KC said. Then she noticed a rounded bulge in the soft leather. She knelt down by the briefcase for a closer look. "I wonder what that is."

Marshall shrugged. "It could be anything," he said. "Like a baseball, Dr. Tutu's lunch . . ."

"Or a priceless hunk of amber with an emerald inside," KC whispered.

7
Please Pass the Pepper

KC reached for the briefcase.

"Um, I don't think we should be doing this," Marshall said.

"Marsh, this is a matter of national security!" KC said. "It's our duty to open the briefcase!"

She turned around to make sure they were alone in the room. Then she flipped the latch on the briefcase. She pulled out the ransom note and a folder with a bunch of papers in it.

She stuck her hand in all the way to feel for the lump.

"Well, did you find it?" Marshall asked.

KC pulled out a big red apple and set it on the table.

"Rats," Marshall said. "I thought we just solved the mystery."

"Not me," KC said. "I'm glad it's not Dr. Tutu!"

KC put the apple back in the briefcase, closed it, and returned it to its spot by the table. Then she went across the hall and peeked through the window again. "He's still sweeping," she told Marshall.

"Can I help you, miss?" a voice asked.

A man was walking up the hall toward her. He was short, with a wrinkled face and a bald head. He was dressed in the same brown shirt and cargo pants that Dirk was wearing. The name JAMIE was stitched over the shirt pocket.

"We're waiting for Dirk," KC said. "He's

in there with the tigers, but he couldn't hear us knock." Then she sneezed.

Jamie looked at KC with piercing green eyes. "You're one of the kids Dr. Tutu has playing with the cubs, right?" he asked.

KC nodded. "We have to ask Dirk something important," she said, fighting back another sneeze. It didn't work. She sneezed again.

Jamie chuckled. "You're allergic to pepper, right?" he asked.

KC's eyes got wide. "Pepper?" she said. "I thought I was allergic to baby tigers!"

Jamie pulled a plastic water pistol from his pocket. "This thing is loaded with pepper and water," he told KC and Marshall. "I carry it in case I run into an animal who wants to play rough. One squirt of this stuff and most of them back off."

"Do Dirk and Dr. Tutu have one, too?" she asked.

"Yep. We all do," Jamie said. "Well, Dr. Tutu doesn't carry his very often."

KC sneezed again.

The man looked through the window. "I guess you can wait for Dirk inside," he said. Jamie pulled a ring of keys from a pocket and stuck one into the door's lock.

"Aren't you afraid of the tiger?" asked Marshall.

"Don't worry, she's behind thick glass," Jamie said. He opened the door and the three of them walked in.

A wall of glass separated them from where Dirk was working. Next to it was a panel of buttons, a telephone, and a tall refrigerator. A monkey magnet held a list of phone numbers on the refrigerator. Set into the glass wall was a door with a lock on the handle. A sign on the door said: DANGER—ZOO EMPLOYEES ONLY—ALL OTHERS STAY OUT.

KC and Marshall watched the baby tigers playing on the other side of the glass. Now that KC and Marshall were inside, they could see more of the tigers' zoo home. There were boulders, terraces, a dark cave, trees and bushes, even a moat with water in it. Dirk still had not noticed the kids or Jamie.

"Where's the mother tiger?" Marshall whispered.

"There's no need to whisper," Jamie said. "This glass is two inches thick. The tigers can't hear us, and even a charging rhino couldn't break through it."

Jamie pointed to the left. "The mother

tiger is in her cave," he said. "But that's behind glass, too. We can move the glass over the cave entrance by pushing that red button. She's locked in her cave while Dirk's cleaning. He's perfectly safe. When he comes back out here, he'll push the blue button to raise the cave glass so mama can join her cubs again."

"Can they see us?" KC asked. She stood as far from Jamie as she could so she wouldn't keep sneezing.

Jamie shook his head. "Nope. The glass is one-way," he said. "We can see Dirk, but he can't see us."

KC pointed to the telephone on the wall. "Can we talk to Dirk?" she asked.

"It's probably best not to bother him," Jamie said. "He should be done in a few minutes. If you want, you can wait right here for him. I have to go see to the lions."

Jamie left, closing the door behind him. Through the thick glass, KC and Marshall watched Dirk while the cubs scampered around his feet.

"So now you know why you've been sneezing," Marshall said. "It wasn't the tigers at all."

KC nodded. "It was Dirk's pepper gun," she said. "I only sneezed when I was around him."

Dirk finished sweeping the tigers' yard. He leaned his broom against a tree and got down on his knees. The two cubs charged him, eager to play. Dirk scooped them up, holding both in one large hand. He used his other hand to tickle them behind their ears.

"That's funny," Marshall said. "Dirk has

a silver bracelet just like that woman's."

"What woman?" KC asked.

"Connie, the lady in the security room," Marshall said.

KC looked closer at the bracelet on Dirk's wrist. Marshall was right. It did look a lot like the one Connie wore. She watched as Dirk lifted the cubs in the air, both in one hand.

"Oh my gosh!" KC gasped. "It's Dirk!"

"Duh, I know it's Dirk," Marshall said.

"No, I mean Dirk is the thief!" KC said. "I just figured it out!"

"And you're going to tell me, right?" Marshall cracked.

"I know how he stole the emerald," KC went on. "When the lights went out, he held both cubs in one hand, like he's doing now. He reached for the box with his free hand, and that's when our hands touched. When the lights came back on, he had a cub in each hand again. Marsh, he must've stuck the emerald under one of the cubs!"

Marshall stared at Dirk through the glass. "So when he brought the cubs over here, he hid the emerald someplace."

"Yes, but he had to do it without Dr. Tutu noticing," KC said. "And I'll bet a million dollars Connie is his partner, and she shut off the lights. She must have been lying when she said she wasn't at the zoo last night."

"How do you figure it was her?" Marshall asked. "Dirk's partner could be anyone."

"Their bracelets match!" KC said. "I'll bet Connie is Dirk's girlfriend."

The kids watched Dirk spread clean straw on the ground.

"So it was Dirk who left the ransom note," Marshall said. "I wonder where he put the emerald."

"Wherever it is, he'll leave it hidden till he gets his ransom money," KC said.

"So what do we do now?" Marshall said. "The cops won't arrest Dirk just because we think he's guilty."

"We have to find the emerald," KC said. She stepped closer to the glass. "It could be anywhere in the enclosure."

"Yeah, like under that straw, buried in the ground, even in the tiger cave," Marshall said. "And before you even think about it, I'm not going in there to look!"

"I have a better idea," KC said. She reached for the telephone.

8
Matching Bracelets

"Who are you calling?" Marshall asked.

"Him," KC said, nodding toward Dirk. She glanced at the list of phone numbers on the refrigerator.

"What? You're calling Dirk?" Marshall squawked. "Are you nuts? He'll feed us to the tigers!"

KC shook her head. "Dirk won't know who's calling," she said. "He can't see us through this one-way glass, remember?"

KC dialed Dirk's cell phone number.

They watched him unclip his cell phone from his belt and flip it open. "Hello?"

KC felt weird talking to Dirk this way.

She could see him, but he had no idea where his caller was calling from.

"Hello, Dirk," KC said, disguising her voice so she sounded older.

"Who's this?" Dirk asked.

"A friend," KC said. She made a face at Marshall.

KC watched Dirk lean his broom against a tree. "Yeah? I have a lot of friends. You got a name?"

"I have some information for you," KC said.

Marshall shook his head at KC.

"You do, huh? Listen, lady, I don't like salespeople, and I don't buy stuff over the phone," Dirk said.

KC almost laughed. "I'm not selling anything," she said. "I know you and Connie stole the emerald." KC's heart was beating a jillion times a minute. She could feel sweat making the phone slippery in her hand.

Dirk didn't say anything. But he didn't end the conversation, either.

"I know you put the ransom note under Dr. Tutu's door," KC went on. "But you're not getting that million dollars. You're going to share it with me."

KC and Marshall saw Dirk yank the phone away from his ear as if it had bitten him. He looked at the phone, then glanced around the tiger enclosure.

"Keep talking," Dirk said into his phone.

"Don't worry, I will," KC said. "And by the way, I have the emerald. I found where you hid it. If you don't give me half the ransom, the emerald goes to the cops. And I tell them all about how you and your girlfriend planned the whole thing. I'll call you later and tell you where to leave my half million dollars."

KC hung up the phone. Her hand was shaking. "I feel a little sick," she said.

"Think how *he* feels!" Marshall said, pointing to Dirk.

Dirk stared at his cell phone. He stood perfectly still with the phone in his hand. Finally he flipped it shut and clipped it back onto his belt.

On the other side of the glass, KC crossed her fingers. "Come on, Dirk," she whispered. "Show us where you hid it."

After a moment, Dirk walked toward the moat. He knelt down and plunged his arm into the water, up to his elbow. Checking to make sure he wasn't being watched, he pulled his arm out.

KC gasped. Dirk was holding the Tiger's Eye in his dripping hand.

"You did it!" Marshall cried.

"Quick, Marsh, lock the door!" yelled KC. She reached for the phone again.

Twenty minutes later, KC and Marshall stood with some other tourists outside the tiger enclosure. The mother tiger was cooling off in the moat. Her two cubs played with a soccer ball nearby.

KC had finally gotten through to the president's private phone. When she told him how she'd tricked Dirk, he sent the police to the zoo.

"Come on, we have to meet the president," KC said. "He's bringing Dr. Tutu and Mr. Chu."

Olmstead Walk wound through the zoo

past many of the animal enclosures. KC and Marshall passed the reptile center and the ape house. A few minutes later, they walked onto the porch on the front of Dr. Tutu's office. He was serving glasses of lemonade to Sunwoo, her father, and the president.

"You're just in time," Dr. Tutu said. He passed KC and Marshall each a glass.

Just then three police officers walked past, leading Dirk and Connie toward the exit gate.

"Look, KC," Marshall whispered. "They're wearing matching handcuffs!"

"You are very smart!" Sunwoo said to KC and Marshall. "How did you know that man was the thief?"

"I didn't know anything!" Marshall laughed. "KC figured it out and called his cell phone. I just stood there shaking."

Everyone looked at KC. She blushed. "It had to be Dirk," she said. "Once we knew that the Tiger's Eye was hidden outside the party room, the rest was easy. Dirk dropped it into the moat when he took the cubs back to the enclosure. He was the only one who could have done that."

"Mr. Chu has agreed to let the zoo keep the Tiger's Eye for a year," the president said. He looked at Dr. Tutu. "Where will it be displayed?"

"Someplace near the tigers," Dr. Tutu said. "Right, Mr. Chu?"

Sunwoo's father nodded. "Yes. People will come to see the tigers. They will also see the Tiger's Eye and read its history. This will be a good thing for the tigers."

Mr. Chu winked at KC and Marshall. "It has already brought luck!"

Did you know?

Did you know that the Sumatran tiger cubs that KC and Marshall met will grow to weigh about 300 pounds? They also have webbed feet and love to swim. But Sumatran tigers are critically endangered, which means that there are very few of them living in the wild—fewer than 500, in fact.

Luckily, there are many people who want to help the tigers. Zoos like the National Zoo do a lot of work to save Sumatran tigers and other endangered species from going extinct. They make sure the tigers in the zoo are healthy. They give them a safe place to have babies. And they work with local people in Asia to find ways to live near the tigers in peace.

The National Zoo has been doing work like this for all kinds of animals for over a century! When it first opened in 1889, North American animals like bison and beavers were quickly disappearing. The zoo was a safe place for them to live. Over the years, many more species of animals all over the world became threatened. Helping endangered animals became a main goal for the zoo.

Today at the National Zoo, you can see nearly 400 different species of animals. Anyone can visit for free. If you are too far away to visit in person, you can visit anytime on the Internet. Just go to nationalzoo.si.edu. You can even see the Sumatran tigers live on their Tigercam!

A to Z Mysteries®

Help Dink, Josh, and Ruth Rose . . .

. . . solve mysteries
from A to Z!

Random House